*In tribute to Rose Fitzgerald Kennedy,*
*a woman who planted her own perennial garden*

Copyright © 2009 by Peter H. Reynolds

First edition 2009

Library of Congress Cataloging-in-Publication Data

Reynolds, Peter, date.
Rose's garden / Peter H. Reynolds. — 1st ed.
p.    cm.
Summary: Rose finds a neglected patch of earth in the middle of a bustling city where
she can plant the flower seeds collected from her travels in her magical teapot.
ISBN 978-0-7636-4641-7
[1. Flowers — Fiction.  2. Gardens — Fiction.]
I. Title.
PZ7.R337645Rg 2010
[E] — dc22     2009024175

09 10 11 12 13 14 LBM 10 9 8 7 6 5 4 3 2 1

Printed in Melrose Park, IL, U.S.A.

This book was typeset in Cochin.
The illustrations were done in watercolor and ink.

Candlewick Press
99 Dover Street
Somerville, Massachusetts 02144

visit us at www.candlewick.com

To learn more about Rose Fitzgerald Kennedy and the Greenway in Boston
that bears her name, and to see an animated digital storybook version of
*Rose's Garden*, go to www.rosekennedygreenway.org.

# ROSE'S GARDEN

## Peter H. Reynolds

CANDLEWICK PRESS

Rose was a dreamer.
An adventurer.
She explored the world in her fantastic teapot.

Rose collected seeds from each place
she visited to remember it by.

The teapot became heavy and brimmed with seeds.

"It is time to plant my garden."

There in the distance was a big, bustling city by the sea.

"Welcome, friend. Sail upriver. It's lovely there,"
the harbormaster called down to Rose.

"Thank you. I think I'll explore the city first," said Rose.

She soon found herself
in the busiest part of the city.

And there she spotted a dusty, forgotten stretch of earth.

*Hmmm,* Rose pondered. *This little patch needs some color.*

Rose began preparing the soil, imagining what
a different, colorful place this could be.

When she went to gather her seeds from the teapot,
she noticed a flock of birds flying away from it.

The birds seemed full and happy.

"Oh, no!"

Rose slipped into the teapot and carefully gathered
the few remaining seeds.

She tucked them inside her pocket, then hurried from the dock.

Rose planted her seeds and waited. Patiently.

But nothing seemed to happen.

The rains of spring made the soil too wet.

The heat of summer made the ground too dry.

The chill of autumn came too early.

She waited through the snowy winter.

The snow melted. The ground warmed.
Still Rose waited—determined that her seeds would awaken.

Word spread of Rose's faith in her garden.

One warm spring day, a girl approached Rose with a gift.
It was a paper flower.

"I made it myself, for your garden," the girl said, beaming.
"Thank you!" said Rose.

The next day, a boy appeared with his own hand-crafted flower.

Rose was delighted.
"This will be in good company when my own flowers bloom!"

Day after day, more children came to visit,
each with a paper flower.

Each told a story about coming to this city . . . having journeyed
from all over the world, like seeds carried on a breeze.

Before long, the garden was filled with color . . . glorious color.
Thousands of flowers—each one made of paper.
Rose marveled.

As she waded among them, she heard a sound. A buzzing.
She noticed a bee gently land on one of the flowers.
She peered closer. This flower was not made of paper!

She breathed in its sweet perfume.

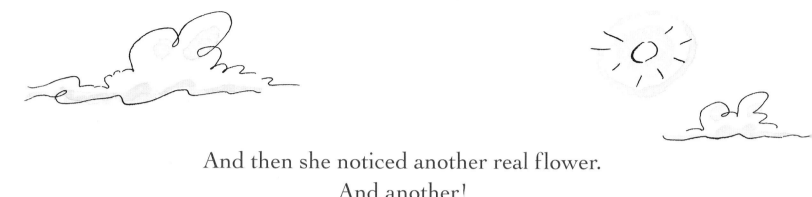

And then she noticed another real flower.
And another!

Each flower, real or paper, had appeared around her
because Rose believed. Her faith had gathered a garden—
and the stories of a city.

Rose realized then that her travels were over. She was home.
Home, in this amazing garden—this splash of color in the middle
of a great city. Surrounded by stories and flowers.

Here in Rose's garden.
Everybody's garden.